**SPORTS INJURIES:
HOW TO PREVENT, DIAGNOSE, & TREAT**

BASEBALL

Sports Injuries:
How to Prevent, Diagnose, & Treat

- Baseball
- Basketball
- Cheerleading
- Equestrian
- Extreme Sports
- Field
- Field Hockey
- Football
- Gymnastics
- Hockey
- Ice Skating
- Lacrosse
- Soccer
- Track
- Volleyball
- Weight Training
- Wrestling

SPORTS INJURIES:
HOW TO PREVENT, DIAGNOSE, & TREAT

BASEBALL

JOHN WRIGHT

MASON CREST PUBLISHERS
www.masoncrest.com

Mason Crest Publishers Inc.
370 Reed Road
Broomall, PA 19008
(866) MCP-BOOK (toll free)
www.masoncrest.com

Copyright © 2004 Mason Crest Publishers, Inc.

All rights reserved. No part of this publication may be reproduced or transmitted in any form or by any means, electronic or mechanical, including photocopying, recording, taping, or any information storage and retrieval system, without permission in writing from the publisher.

First printing

1 2 3 4 5 6 7 8 9 10

Library of Congress Cataloging-in-Publication Data on file
at the Library of Congress

ISBN 1-59084-626-5

Series ISBN 1-59084-625-7

Editorial and design by
Amber Books Ltd.
Bradley's Close
74–77 White Lion Street
London N1 9PF
www.amberbooks.co.uk

Project Editor: Michael Spilling
Design: Graham Curd
Picture Research: Natasha Jones

Printed and bound in the Hashemite Kingdom of Jordan

PICTURE CREDITS
Corbis: 10–11, 12, 15, 18, 20, 23, 24, 29, 33, 34, 36, 37, 45, 49, 51, 52, 54, 56, 57, 58; ©**EMPICS**: 6, 8, 13, 26, 41; **ImageDJ**: 16, 39, 40, 42, 55.

FRONT COVER: All Corbis, except ©EMPICS (tr).

ILLUSTRATIONS: Courtesy of Amber Books except:
Bright Star Publishing plc: 46, 48;
Tony Randell: 30, 31.

IMPORTANT NOTICE

This book is intended to provide general information about sports injuries, their prevention, and their treatment. The information contained herein is not intended as a substitute for professional medical care. Always consult a doctor before beginning any exercise program, and for diagnosis and treatment of any injury. Accordingly, the publisher cannot accept any responsibility for any prosecution or proceedings brought or instituted against any person or body as a result of the use or misuse of the techniques and information within.

CONTENTS

Foreword	6
The History of Baseball	8
Softball—the Other Game	18
Keeping Fit to Avoid Injury	24
Protective Equipment	34
Injuries and Treatment	42
Careers in Baseball	52
Glossary	60
Further Information	62
Index	64

Foreword

Sports Injuries: How to Prevent, Diagnose, and Treat is a seventeen-volume series written for young people who are interested in learning about various sports and how to participate in them safely. Each volume examines the history of the sport and the rules of play; it also acts as a guide for prevention and treatment of injuries, and includes instruction on stretching, warming up, and strength training, all of which can help players avoid the most common musculoskeletal injuries. *Sports Injuries* offers ways for readers to improve their performance and gain more enjoyment from playing sports, and young athletes will find these volumes informative and helpful in their pursuit of excellence.

Sports medicine professionals assigned to a sport that they are not familiar with can also benefit from this series. For example, a football athletic trainer may need to provide medical care for a local gymnastics meet. Although the emergency medical principles and action plan would remain the same, the athletic trainer could provide better care for the gymnasts after reading a simple overview of the principles of gymnastics in *Sports Injuries*.

Although these books offer an overview, they are not intended to be comprehensive in the recognition and management of sports injuries. The text helps the reader appreciate and gain awareness of the common injuries possible during participation in sports. Reference material and directed readings are provided for those who want to delve further into the subject.

Written in a direct and easily accessible style, *Sports Injuries* is an enjoyable series that will help young people learn about sports and sports medicine.

Susan Saliba, Ph.D., National Athletic Trainers' Association Education Council

The New York Yankees celebrate a victory over the New York Mets in the 2000 World Series.

The History of Baseball

If someone mentions "America's favorite pastime" or "our national game," you know the subject is baseball. True, football is equally popular and basketball is the only world-famous sport invented in the United States, but because it is our first popular game, baseball has a special place in the nation's heart.

Baseball's season begins in the springtime and lingers through the warm summer months and on into the fall. Americans created it from an English school game called **rounders**, which has been played since the 1700s. Indeed, one English alphabet book published in 1744 even listed it under "B" for "base ball." Rounders is more like softball, using a softer ball that is pitched underhand. Only two "bases" were originally used, marked by poles instead of bags. Players were called out if the opposing team threw the ball and hit them as they were running to first base or between bases, so only a soft ball would do.

Some early American versions of baseball had different names, such as "old cat," "goal ball," "town ball," and the "Massachusetts game." One of the main developers of the U.S. game was Abner Doubleday, who laid out a baseball field in 1839 in Cooperstown, New York, and played one of the first official games. (Appropriately, the National Baseball Hall of Fame is now located in Cooperstown.) Doubleday,

Eric Karros of the Los Angeles Dodgers is a major league star who has special athletic skills and provides exciting action for America's baseball fans.

who has even been given credit for "inventing" baseball, later became a Union general during the Civil War and was a hero at the Battle of Gettysburg.

The first basic rules for our modern-day game were drawn up in New York in 1845 by a number of individuals, including Alexander Cartwright, a surveyor. Throwing the ball at the runner was outlawed for the first time. Such amateur New York teams as the Knickerbockers, Gothams, and Empires used these rules for their 1846 season. Soldiers playing in camps during the Civil War spread this version around the country.

Professional teams appeared when the war ended in 1865, and the National Association of Professional Baseball Players was established in 1870. Its teams

"Take me out to the ballgame" is the cry heard during the spring and summer in the major and minor league parks of the nation, such as Chicago's famous Wrigley Field.

included two familiar names—the White Stockings of Chicago and the Athletics of Philadelphia—but many did not survive, for example, the Kekiongas of Fort Wayne, Indiana; Forest Cities of Cleveland, Ohio; Mutuals of New York; and Eckfords of Brooklyn. The association broke up in 1876 when the National League of Professional Base Ball Clubs formed. The American Association began as a rival in 1891 and later became the American League. The two "major leagues" were now in place, and the World Series began in 1903.

THE STARS

The first half of the twentieth century produced great stars of the game, whose names increased baseball's popularity, contributing to its lasting success. The pride of the New York Yankees included "Babe" Ruth, Lou Gehrig, and Joe DiMaggio, while

"BABE" RUTH (1895–1948)

George Herman "Babe" Ruth has been called "the most dominant player in history." His record of sixty home runs in one season (1927) was not broken until 1961 (when seasons had themselves become longer), and his career record of 714 lasted until 1974, when Hank Aaron hit his 715th home run.

Ruth began as a pitcher with the Boston Red Sox, pitching 29 2/3 scoreless World Series innings for them. But the Babe was such a powerful hitter that he was shifted to the outfield, meaning that he could bat in every game. The New York Yankees bought him in 1920 for $125,000, which proved a wise investment. His fourteen seasons of home runs earned him the title of "the Sultan of Swat," and Yankee Stadium is still called "the house that Ruth built."

During his career, Ruth scored 2,174 runs and batted in 2,211 more. His batting average of .847 in 1920 is still the record. He was so dangerous at the plate that pitchers walked him a record 2,056 times. Ruth retired in 1935.

Babe Ruth, baseball's famous hitter, began his brilliant career as a successful Red Sox pitcher, winning 94 games.

The USA Olympic team celebrates winning the gold medal at the 2000 Sydney games, after upsetting Cuba 4–0. Cuba won baseball gold medals in 1992 and 1996.

the St. Louis Cardinals had Rogers Hornsby, "Dizzy" Dean, and Stan Musial. Among many other famous players were Ty Cobb of the Detroit Tigers, Ted Williams of the Boston Red Sox, and Jackie Robinson of the Brooklyn Dodgers. As the century closed, famous players kept coming, including Barry Bonds of the San Francisco Giants, Mark McGwire of St. Louis, Sammy Sosa of the Chicago Cubs, Randy Johnson of the Arizona Diamondbacks, and Roger Clemens of the Toronto Blue Jays.

Equally impressive have been baseball's successful managers. In New York alone, Joe McGraw guided the Giants to ten National League pennants and three

World Series victories from 1902 to 1932; Joe McCarthy's Yankee teams won seven World Series between 1932 and 1943; and Casey Stengel led the Yankees to seven titles, including five straight from 1949 to 1953. Colorful managers have included the Giants' tough Leo Durocher, known as "Leo the Lip," who warned, "Nice guys finish last."

Amateur baseball has also continued to be strong, with special growth in the number of youth teams in such leagues as the Little League and the Babe Ruth League (see Chapter 6). Baseball is now played around the world. A baseball exhibition game at the 1936 Olympics in Berlin, Germany, drew 125,000 spectators. The first Olympic Gold Medal was won by Cuba at the 1992 games in Barcelona, Spain; and the U.S. team took gold at the 2000 Olympics in Sydney, Australia.

THE BASIC RULES

A team has nine players, and each game lasts nine innings. The visiting team bats first in the "top half" of each inning, and then plays defense while the home team bats in the "bottom half." If tied after regulation play, the game continues until one side is ahead after any extra inning.

The bases, or bags, are at the corners of a square that makes up the infield "diamond," and there is a distance of 90 feet (27.4 m) between each base. The pitcher stands in the center on the "mound," which is elevated 10 inches (25 cm), and delivers pitches to each batter at home plate, which is $60\frac{1}{2}$ feet (18.4 m) from the mound. The ball itself has a circumference of about 9 inches (23 cm) and the bat a maximum length of 42 inches (107 cm). A batter tries to hit the ball far enough—hopefully into the outfield—to advance to one or more bases. If four pitches are thrown outside the batter's **strike zone**, the batter receives a free "walk" to first base. A batter hit by a pitch can also go to first base.

JACKIE ROBINSON (1919–1972)

Major league baseball had no African-American players until 1947, the year Jackie Robinson joined the Brooklyn Dodgers at second base. It was a good move because Robinson was named Rookie of the Year, and two years later he became the National League's Most Valuable Player. He played on six pennant-winning teams in his ten years with Brooklyn, including the 1955 World Series championship team.

Jackie Robinson goes for a double play as Hank Sauer of the Chicago Cubs slides into second during a 1952 game.

Born in Cairo, Georgia, Robinson played four sports at UCLA before signing in 1946 with Brooklyn and being assigned to the Dodgers' farm team in Montreal, Canada, where he led the league in batting. Moving up to Brooklyn the next year, he proved an excellent hitter, achieving a career batting average of .311. He was also a daring base runner, twice leading the league in stolen bases and stealing home nineteen times.

After he retired in 1956, Robinson turned to politics, particularly the Civil Rights Movement. In 1962, he became the first African American named to the Baseball Hall of Fame.

Runs are scored when a player moves around the bases, returning to home plate. A ball hit inbounds over a fence is a home run, which lets the batter make a free circuit of the bases. The batting side is retired after three outs in an inning. A player can be called out for several reasons:

- letting three good pitches go by, either swinging and missing or not swinging—known as a strikeout;
- hitting a ball that is thrown to first base before the player can run there—thrown out;
- hitting a ball that is caught in the air by a defensive player—fly out;
- running between bases and being touched with the ball by a defensive player—tagged out;

Stealing a base is one of the most difficult and exciting baseball plays. Some players with speed and quick reflexes have become base-stealing specialists.

MARK McGWIRE (1963–)

"I can't believe I did that," said the St. Louis Cardinal's Mark McGwire on September 27, 1998. "It blows my mind. I am almost speechless. I've amazed myself." In fact, he amazed everyone, for McGwire had just hit his seventieth home run of the season in his last game, breaking the seasonal record set thirty-seven years earlier by Roger Maris of the New York Yankees.

"Big Mac," who stands 6 ft 5 in (1.95 m) and weighs 250 lb (113 kg), had joined the Oakland Athletics in 1986, becoming the American League Rookie of the Year and helping the Athletics to win the 1989 World Series. Oakland would regret trading the first baseman to St. Louis in 1997, when he blasted fifty-eight home runs, a year before the record seventy.

McGwire, however, began to have injury troubles. In 2000, he missed games because of a back injury, and the next year went zero for twenty-nine at bats while recovering from knee surgery. Still, big McGwire has assured his superstar status. As the Cardinal manager, Tony La Russa, said of McGwire's abilities after his seventieth home run: "He's stranger than fiction."

- having to advance to the next base because another runner is behind and a defensive player with the ball touches the base first—forced out.

The defensive infield players are the pitcher, catcher, first baseman, second baseman, shortstop (between second and third bases), and third baseman. The three outfield players are the left fielder, center fielder, and right fielder.

Softball — the Other Game

Softball has more players than any other U.S. team sport, with more than forty million people playing the game during the summer months. Like baseball, it is an exciting game of skill, but its smaller playing field makes it even faster.

Softball also has other advantages: Boys, girls, men, and women of any age can play; the equipment and uniforms cost little; and amateur leagues can be quickly formed by schools, churches, and businesses. It is an ideal informal game at picnics and other outings.

The Amateur Softball Association (**ASA**), which is the national governing body of the sport in the United States, has more than 250,000 official member teams with four million players. This includes its youth program of more than 80,000 teams, which has some 1.3 million players ranging from under ten years old up to eighteen.

The game was invented in 1887 on a cold winter day in Chicago, when George Hancock saw someone in the Farragut Boat Club toss an old boxing glove at another person, who hit it right back with a stick. Hancock chalked off a small baseball field in the club's gym, and two teams of friends played the first game of "indoor baseball"; the score was 41–40. The next spring, he organized games

Softball is enjoyed by millions of men, women, and children around the world and has become an Olympic sport. It can be faster than baseball because of the smaller playing field.

A University of Washington softball pitcher winds up for an underhand delivery. The popular college game has expanded into intercollegiate competition.

around Chicago on fields too small for baseball, changed the name to "indoor-outdoor," and drew up nineteen rules that were adopted in 1889 by the Mid Winter Indoor Baseball League of Chicago.

People quickly realized the advantage of a sport that could be played in small public parks and on school playgrounds. Other cities took up the game, especially Minneapolis, where fireman Lewis Rober used a small medicine ball for the games he organized on a vacant lot to keep firemen in good condition during their off hours. His team was nicknamed the Kittens, and the local game became known as "kitten ball" until 1925, when the Minneapolis Park Board renamed it "diamond ball." Other areas called the game "mush ball" and "playground ball." The next year, however, Walter Hakanson, a Denver YMCA official, suggested "softball." By then, the game was well established in Illinois, Minnesota, Wisconsin, Colorado, and Florida.

SOFTBALL GOES OFFICIAL

In 1923, the National Recreation Congress in Springfield, Illinois, began to draw up new official softball rules of play. The nonprofit Amateur Softball Association (ASA) was founded in 1933 in Newark, New Jersey. That same year, it adopted the rules, then quickly organized a tournament that was held at the Chicago World's Fair. Based since 1966 in Oklahoma City, Oklahoma, ASA now has more than eighty levels of play for youths and adult men and women, including teams for men over seventy-five years old. In 1973, it dedicated a National Softball Hall of Fame, which by 2003 had inducted 126 members, including players, managers, umpires, and administrators. The organization also has a Softball Museum and Hall of Fame Stadium for national tournaments.

Like baseball, the amateur game of softball has spread around the world. It was even an Olympic sport in 2000, when the U.S. softball team won the gold medal in Sydney, Australia. The International Softball Federation (ISF) in Plant City, Florida, has member organizations in 124 nations—even China has a Softball Association. The ISF collects and sends used equipment valued at $200,000 a year to overseas teams and holds world championships for men and women. It also has an International Softball Federation Hall of Fame, which had ninety-two members from twenty countries by 2003.

DIFFERENT RULES

Although similar to baseball, softball has important differences. The game is shorter, having only seven innings; the field is smaller, as is the bat, which is a maximum of 34 in (86 cm), or 8 in (20 cm) shorter than the bat used for baseball; and the ball is large, with a circumference of about 12 in (30 cm), or some 3 in (7.5 cm) larger than a baseball. The ball is pitched from a flat area, not a mound. Two types of softball games have also developed, the fast-pitch and slow-pitch versions.

Fast-pitch softball, with nine players, is closer to baseball. However, the ball is pitched underhand, the strike zone extends from the armpits to the knees, and runners can leave their bases only if a pitch has left the pitcher's hand. The distance between bases is 60 ft (18.2 m), and from the pitching rubber to home plate is 46 ft (14 m) for men and 40 ft (12.2 m) for women. Teams are usually single sex.

Soft-pitch softball has ten players, the extra "rover" player being in the outfield. The ball must be pitched higher, 6–12 ft (1.8–3.6 m) above the ground. The strike zone is from the top of the shoulders to the knees. A batter who fouls off a third strike is out. Stealing bases is not allowed, and a player who leaves a base before a pitch reaches the plate or is hit is called out. The distance between bases is 65 ft (19.8 m) and from the pitching plate to home plate is 46 ft (14 m) for both men and women.

Softball looks like baseball, but the ball is larger and the bat is smaller. Local clubs have the attraction of bringing friends together on teams, such as those sponsored by a church or office.

SOFTBALL—THE OTHER GAME

Keeping Fit to Avoid Injury

Baseball and softball injuries are a fact of life, but a player who stays in good condition has a better chance of avoiding major injuries and reducing the minor ones. Three proven ways involve mental preparations, pregame warm-ups, and year-round conditioning programs.

As in all sports, positive motivation can give a player the extra strength needed for victory. If you are convinced that you are well-prepared and you are confident of winning, the game is almost won. We all can tell when a team is "up" for a game, being inspired to play better than normal. Perhaps their motivation comes from the fact that this is a crucial contest, or they wish to avenge a previous defeat or win for a retiring coach. Whatever the reason, the players are mentally fired up.

This mental conditioning is also used by baseball and softball players to play a safer game. The technique, known as **visualization**, helps reduce nervousness and increase confidence. If you are a pitcher who will be facing a dangerous batter, for instance, you can visualize striking your opponent out with a clever mixture of your best pitches. You can also imagine making your best moves on the field without being reckless and inviting injuries. Rehearse in your mind the times that you have slid safely into home plate, handled a line drive in the infield, or leaped

Baseball superstar Mark McGwire holds the two ends of a baseball bat to stretch his upper back muscles before taking up position at home plate.

BASEBALL

Warming up helps a player gain more flexibility, an important attribute for baseball, as seen in this jump by New York Yankee Derek Jeter over a Toronto base runner.

and thrown over a runner at second to complete a **double play**. Remember that you can build up a positive self-image by controlling your attitudes and emotions.

Sports psychologists say negative thinking or a bad attitude can actually cause injuries. If you control anxiety and anger, you will play better and safer. This is so important that professional baseball teams have sports psychologists on their staffs who work with players on mental conditioning. Most players, of course, do not have such professional help and must rely on themselves and on pep talks with other team members to learn how to relax, gain confidence, reduce stress, and avoid injuries.

Visualization, or mental imagery, is especially important and can be practiced days or hours before a game. Find a time and place to relax, then picture yourself in a game, remembering the way the stadium looks and the views and sounds that you will experience from your position on the field: the grass, the **bullpen**, the

GEORGE BRETT (1953–)

The Kansas City Royals were fortunate to have George Brett for his entire twenty-year major league career. In the 1970s and 1980s, he led them to six American League pennants and two World Series, winning the title in 1985. He batted over .300 for ten seasons and led the league three times, including a .390 average in 1980. When he took the batting title in 1990, he became the first major league player in history to win it in three different decades.

Brett would have filled more of the record book if he had stayed healthy. His numerous injuries kept him on the disabled list for more than thirty-two weeks from 1978 to 1989. Even during his spectacular 1980 season, he suffered with tendonitis, a bruised heel, and torn ligaments. He retired from the game in 1993, the year that he became only the third player in baseball history to make three thousand hits, three hundred home runs, and two hundred stolen bases. He was inducted into the Hall of Fame in 1999.

scoreboard, the **dugout** chatter, even the fans roaring their approval at your play. Imagine hitting a homer into the bleachers, stealing a base, or catching a fly ball against the outfield fence to retire the team at bat.

Injuries will also be fewer when you increase your concentration during the game. Whether batting or playing defense, you can be both "psyched up" and calm at the same time. This "relaxed attention" can be increased by talking to yourself: "Here comes his fast ball," "Watch out for the **bunt**," "He'll be running on the next pitch," and so on. You can also hear relaxed chatter among the infield players as they encourage each another. Good players enjoy the competition and are not too anxious and tense about their batting and fielding. They know that it is not the end of the world if they strike out or commit an error. Many more opportunities will come to a well-trained player.

WARMING UP

One of the best ways to prevent baseball or softball injuries is to warm up before each game because cold muscles are more likely to be injured, and stiff muscles cause clumsy play. Increased flexibility will make it easier for you to respond more quickly in a game. Besides warming the muscles, warm-up exercises will stretch them, as well as the **ligaments** and connective tissues. Such exercises are also **aerobic**, so your heart and respiratory rates will also increase, supplying additional oxygen to your body's system. Even a warm-up of five to ten minutes will have a positive effect. This could include simple walking or running in place, followed by jumping jacks. We are also familiar with players warming up at their positions on the field: players making relaxed throws around the infield, pitchers tossing the ball in the bullpen, and upcoming batters swinging in the on-deck circle.

Stretching is very important, and each major muscle group needs a pregame

KEEPING FIT TO AVOID INJURY

Ken Griffey of the Cincinnati Reds warms up in the on-deck circle before batting. Besides pregame warm-ups, players should stretch after sitting out their half of the inning.

workout. Throwing is the movement most used in the games of baseball and softball; pitchers, catchers, infielders, and outfielders must all protect their throwing arms. To help avoid sore arms and injuries, try these stretching exercises:

- Let one arm hang loosely next to the body. Then take the elbow with your other hand and pull the arm until the biceps touch your chin. Hold for five to ten seconds. Then change arms and repeat. Do this two or three times for each arm.
- Place one arm on the back of your head, then put your other hand on the top of the elbow, and pull it lightly for five to ten seconds. Switch arms and repeat. Again, do this two or three times for each arm.

Throwing is also the most common pregame warm-up done on the field:

- Two players stand 25–40 feet (7.6–12.1 m) apart and toss the ball back and forth about a dozen times—use a big circle movement of the arm in order to stretch the shoulder and **rotator cuff**. Increase the distance to 45–65 feet (13.7–19.8 m) for twelve more throws, and finally 80–100 feet (24–30 m) for about ten throws. Players who are twelve years old or younger should not throw at this longer distance, which might cause injuries.

Pitchers can warm up with fifteen to twenty-five throws before a game, but at no longer a distance than their regular

To help keep their muscles warm and flexible, players should jog back onto the field, rather than walk.

To stretch your hamstring muscles, sit on the floor with your back straight. Slowly bend forward to grasp your ankles; hold the stretch for ten to fifteen seconds, then relax.

pitches during a game. It is important to limit the number and types of pitches thrown by a young pitcher. Serious injuries can occur to a player's growth plates, where bone growth occurs near the joints. Too much stress placed on the elbow and shoulder can cause damage, even a chipped bone, which would ruin the possibility of a baseball career. The Little League limits pitchers to one full game (six innings) a week. The American Sports Medicine Institute (ASMI) recommends certain numbers of pitches for young players pitching two games a week: seventy-five for ages thirteen to fourteen; seventy for ages eleven to twelve; and fifty for ages nine to ten.

Pitchers who are aged eleven or under are also advised not to throw **curveballs** as these involve a snapping motion of the wrist and put pressure on the arm, all of which could cause serious damage.

Baseball and softball are games that often require rotating, or twisting, your body in the same direction. Think of a shortstop, who constantly cuts off a ground ball and turns quickly to throw it to first; or a batter swinging at pitches, always from the same side of the plate. Repeating these moves over and over can cause rotational strains and pains. These can be minimized by a warm-up that includes a few light rotation moves, such as holding your hands straight out in front of you and rotating your body in both directions, as if swinging an imaginary bat. Then pick up the bat for easy practice swings in both directions, back and forth. This will warm the muscles on both sides and help avoid a "corkscrew" injury caused by twisting.

Other warm-up exercises could include:

- Sit, then hold up each foot separately while you rotate the ankle—this will help avoid ankle sprains;
- Sit, then reach forward to grasp your ankles—this will help prevent **hamstring** sprains or pulls;
- Stand, then bend the knees, and stand, then touch your toes—these exercises will help avoid back and thigh injuries.

Players should also keep their muscles warm in the dugout when their team is at bat. Walking around a bit is better than sitting out a long half inning. (But do not imitate Rick Honeycutt, a pitcher for four major league teams, who injured his wrist flicking sunflower seeds in the dugout!) And players should briskly jog back onto the field, rather than trudging back to their positions. These small efforts will help to keep players lively and alert when this is needed in the late innings. After a game, players should also do light walking or stretching to help the heart and body gradually slow down.

REGULAR CONDITIONING

A regular physical conditioning program throughout the year will provide additional protection against injuries, such as those caused by overusing muscles.

KEEPING FIT TO AVOID INJURY

The head-first slide is a good tactic by a base runner to beat a throw, but this catcher made the tag anyway. Only experienced players should go into a base head first.

This can be a combination of running, swimming, cycling, and other exercises, such as push-ups, pull-ups, and sit-ups. Aerobic conditioning is needed to avoid fatigue, and strength-and-endurance training can both help reduce injury and promote health. Good strenuous physical activity for twenty to thirty minutes, three days a week, will greatly improve a player's endurance.

Young players, however, should avoid heavy weight training, and all participants need to avoid too much training as the baseball and softball seasons approach. Training that is too long or too vigorous can lead to extra tiredness, stress, and poor performance on the field.

Protective Equipment

Although baseball and softball players stay alert to avoid injuries, the easiest way to have a safe game is to wear protective equipment. The U.S. Consumer Product Safety Commission estimates that more than 58,000 baseball injuries to children, or nearly 36 percent, would be prevented or reduced by wearing proper protective equipment.

The major danger, especially in baseball, is being struck by the ball. Many injuries to young players from a batted, pitched, or thrown ball are due to the player's unskilled response. The standard baseball is made of a core of cork or rubber, which is wound with fibers, such as cotton or wool, and then covered with two pieces of leather sewn together with 108 stitches. It can be pitched at more than 90 miles per hour (145 km/h), so hard that helmets are required for batters in organized leagues. And when hit strongly with a high-tech aluminum bat, the ball may be propelled at far more than 100 miles per hour (160 km/h), so all defensive players must always wear gloves. (In 2002, Americans bought six million baseball gloves.)

The pitcher is in special danger from a batted ball. In 1999, Little League records show that emergency room treatment was needed for twenty-eight injured baseball pitchers and ten softball pitchers, from five to eighteen years

The catcher is the only player on a team in constant danger of being hit by the ball. His lightweight equipment allows freedom of movement to catch a ball thrown at more than 90 miles per hour (145 km/hr).

BASEBALL

Even though he wears the most protective equipment of any player on the field, a catcher can suffer various injuries, from tipped balls to a collision with a runner, which caused this injury.

old. Fortunately, better safety programs have meant that these totals have since fallen. All players should also wear shoes with rubber spikes to reduce injuries.

THE CATCHER'S EQUIPMENT

The catcher occupies the most dangerous position on the field and wears the most protective equipment. Otherwise, he would quickly be injured by foul balls or even a wrongly swung bat. The gear is jokingly called "tools of ignorance" because

PROTECTIVE EQUIPMENT

it supposedly protects him from his own mistakes. As well as the mitt, the catcher's protection should include a helmet, face mask, chest protector, throat protector, shinguards, and a protective supporter cup. All this may look like a burden, but modern equipment is lightweight and provides good freedom of movement.

During a game, the catcher will handle more than 150 pitches. The leather mitt, therefore, is vital for protecting hands and fingers. It should always be worn during practice sessions and warm-ups. The mitt has extra padding and is $15\frac{1}{2}$ inches (39 cm) from top to bottom, which is $3\frac{1}{2}$ inches (9 cm) longer than a fielder's glove. Amateur players should never use a fielder's glove if they are playing catcher.

The catcher's helmet and face mask are light but strong. A helmet usually has vinyl on the outside and leather inside. The masks have a steel framework, and some newer ones are made of a new resin compound advertised to be stronger than steel. Both versions of mask can be flipped up.

The mask is on properly when it is squarely over the face and tightened with the adjustable straps. Individual "goat's beard" throat protectors can be attached to hang from the bottom, but many masks have a built-in wire extension that is 2 inches (5 cm) long. Some have side deflectors built in for extra ear protection.

As with the glove, helmets and masks should always be worn during a practice or warm-up. The catcher's long-style padded chest protector

The catcher's strong but lightweight helmet and face mask are his most vital equipment. The steel mask must also provide the best possible visibility.

covers the upper chest, abdomen, groin, collarbone, and lower neck. Shinguards should fit perfectly to protect from bruises, so catchers should wear their baseball shoes when choosing guards to make sure they are the correct length. A shinguard should cover the kneecap, shinbone, and lower leg, and also have wings to protect the ankle and feet. Most versions add an extended instep plate.

PLATE UMPIRES, BATTERS, AND FIELDERS

Similar additional protective equipment is worn by the plate umpire, who stands directly behind the catcher. This includes a padded body protector, now normally worn underneath the shirt, which covers the chest, shoulders, and upper arms. The umpire's mask needs to provide protection to the side of the head and the throat. It should also offer excellent visibility, enabling the umpire to make accurate decisions.

Batter's helmet

The first protective helmets for batters were worn in 1938, and today's batters are required to wear them. The plastic shell has foam padding inside and extends to cover the ears. The helmet should fit snugly on the head without the back rim resting on the neck, and the bill should not be too low on the forehead because that would block the player's vision. Ordinary baseball caps should not be worn under helmets.

The batting helmet does not, however, protect the face. Youth baseball and softball players have more facial, eye, and mouth injuries than players in any other sport. Safer versions of helmets are available and include either a wire face mask or a transparent plastic shield to cover the face from the tip of the nose to below the chin. This extra protection for the face is required by the Dixie Youth Baseball

PROTECTIVE EQUIPMENT

The hard batting helmet was introduced to the game in 1938. Before that, players wore their soft baseball caps in the batting box and suffered many more head injuries.

BASEBALL

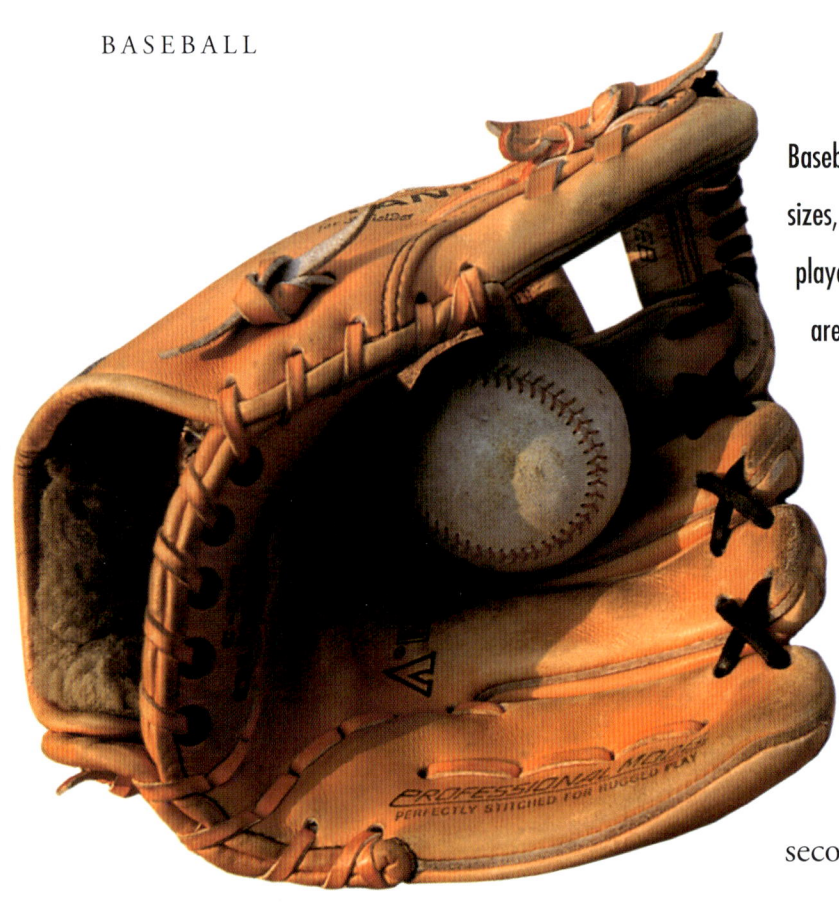

Baseball gloves come in several different sizes, depending on the position of the player. Even special right-handed gloves are available.

organization. Batters can also add plastic goggles, custom-fitted mouth guards, forearm and wrist guards, ankle guards, and shock absorbers worn over the second and middle fingers.

Fielders' gloves

Fielders' gloves measure about 12 inches (30 cm) long and are 8 inches (20 cm) wide. The infielders' gloves are slightly smaller because of the quick play required, but the first baseman has a longer webbing to snag fast throws. Fielders also protect their eyes by wearing sports goggles

OTHER SAFETY EQUIPMENT

A safety-release base may help prevent the injuries caused in organized play when younger players slide into bases—every year, more than 6,600 players are injured in this way. The safety-release base is anchored to rubber mats, and, if it receives a hard knock, it will pop away, leaving no parts sticking out of the ground and no holes in the ground.

PROTECTIVE EQUIPMENT

BASEBALL BATS

"The first step to hitting," said Mickey Mantle, the Yankee's famous hitter, "is to find the right bat." And there are many choices. The famous Louisville Slugger was first made in 1884, and in 2003 the company produced 1.4 million of them for professional and amateur players.

Professional teams must use wooden bats, which are shaped, sanded, and given a natural or flame-burned finish. These have traditionally been made of white ash, but recent years have seen a trend toward maple or a combination of the two. Maple bats do not break as easily and they hit farther. Barry Bonds of the Giants used maple to hit his record seventy-three home runs in 2001.

A bat of any type of wood looks good in the hands of Cliff Floyd of the Florida Marlins.

Light and long-hitting aluminum bats were first used by the Little League in 1971 and have been popular since the 1980s with teams in youth leagues, high schools, and colleges. If professionals switched to them, however, players would score so many home runs that the stadiums would have to be expanded.

Injuries and Treatment

More injuries happen in baseball and softball than in even the high-contact sports of football, basketball, and hockey. One reason, of course, is that more people play on the diamond and face many chances of being hit by the ball, which is the most frequent cause of serious injury and even death.

Every year nearly 500,000 injuries related to baseball are treated in emergency rooms, physicians' offices, clinics, and hospitals. This does not even include those unreported "minor injuries" such as bruises, cuts, and sprains, which are treated with first aid by a coach, player, or parent.

As mentioned, many injuries can be prevented by a physical-conditioning program, warming up before playing, staying alert during the game, and by wearing the proper protective equipment. The fast action of the game, however, ensures that some injuries will result from even the simplest plays, such as throwing the ball or rounding a base. The most important thing is not to ignore the pain, so that you can receive immediate treatment and determine whether the injury is serious.

The most common baseball and softball injuries happen to the shoulders and arms because a player must make so many throws. Injuries also occur to the head, knees, and ankles when players collide, runners slide into bases, and fielders dive

Injuries are a part of the game. Although facing the possibility of being hit by a fast-moving ball, catchers statistically suffer fewer injuries than outfield players because of the protective equipment they wear.

BASEBALL SLANG

Baseball has more colorful language than any other U.S. sport. Someone "out in left field," for instance, is considered to be wrong or sort of strange, because left field was once thought to be less active than center or right field. Here is some more slang:

- Annie Oakley—a free pass to a game, so named because the punched ticket is like a card shot full of holes by the markswoman Annie Oakley
- Baltimore chop—a hit that bounces in front of home plate and hops over an infielder's head
- basket catch—a fielder's catch made by holding the glove upward near belt level
- circus catch—a difficult and spectacular catch by a fielder
- fireman—a relief pitcher who enters the game late to put out any chance of the other team catching up
- hot-stove league—groups of fans who gossip and debate about baseball during the off-season
- payoff—the deciding pitch made when the count is three balls and two strikes
- slap hitter—a batter who tends to hit to all sides of the field
- Texas Leaguer—a soft hit that drops between an infielder and outfielder; also called a "blooper"
- twin killing—a double play

INJURIES AND TREATMENT

to make catches. Fractures are common, and many different bones—from fingertips to legs—are cracked, shattered, or broken.

SHOULDER AND ARM

Injuries to the throwing shoulder are very common. During a professional baseball season, about one-third of the players on the disabled list have shoulder injuries, and in some years these have caused a total of 6,000 missed days of play. The injury might be described as **tendonitis**, inflammation, or strain, and is an **overuse injury** caused by throwing the ball over and over. As a result, a shoulder

The New York Yankees' legendary slugger Mickey Mantle receives a shoulder injury colliding with the Milwaukee Braves' second baseman in the 1957 World Series.

45

SHOULDER INJURIES

Baseball is a throwing game, and shoulder injuries have put many players on the disabled list. This is usually caused by overuse, but also by collisions and being hit by the ball.

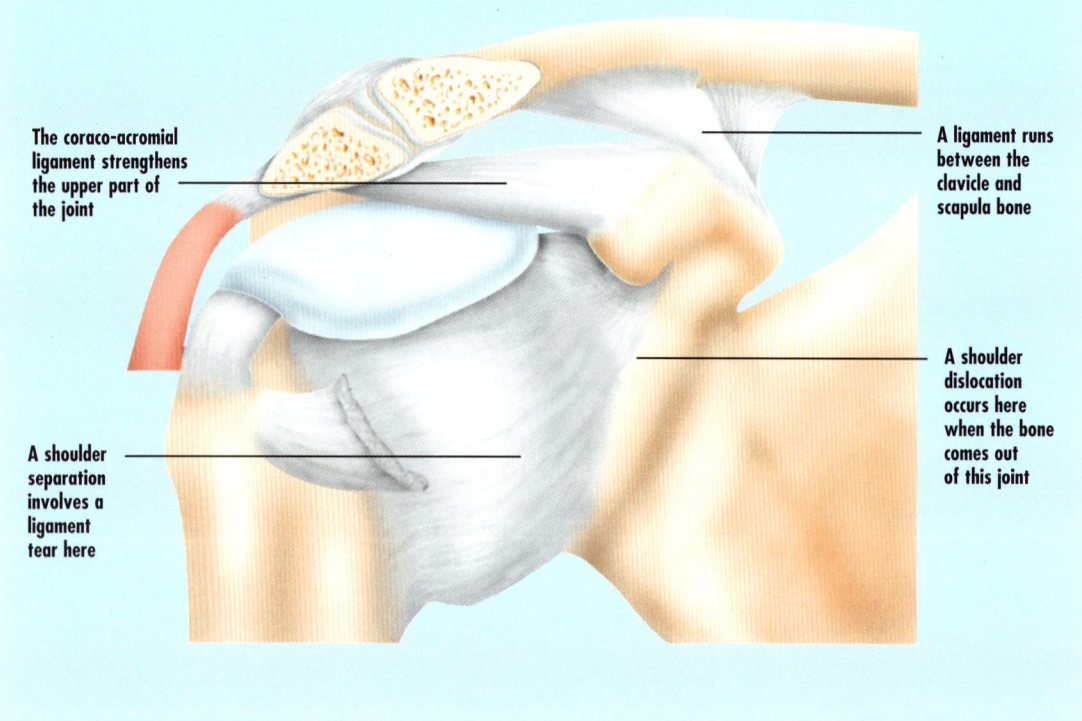

The coraco-acromial ligament strengthens the upper part of the joint

A ligament runs between the clavicle and scapula bone

A shoulder separation involves a ligament tear here

A shoulder dislocation occurs here when the bone comes out of this joint

pain may come and go for a while, and then become progressively worse. Tendonitis means inflammation and pain in the **tendons**, those tough, fibrous tissues that connect muscles and bones. Baseball players, especially pitchers, often get rotator cuff tendonitis when the tendon tears by rubbing the under part of the shoulder. The rotator cuff is the capsule of tendons and muscles that surround the upper arm and holds the shoulder together. Injuries cause pain on the outside of the shoulder, with pain and weakness when lifting the arm.

Young players, who are still growing, should not ignore pain in the shoulder because the stress of throwing can damage the **cartilage** where growth occurs. A player can even fracture the growth plate in the shoulder or suffer a shoulder separation, which is a serious ligament tear in which the end of the collar bone, or clavicle, rises up. Any of these problems require X-rays and can be treated successfully by rest from the game, physical therapy, or, in the worst case, minor surgery.

Little league elbow is another type of stress damage caused by constant throwing. It is important to recognize the symptoms—such as a twinge, tightening, or burning sensation in the muscle—early. It occurs just below the elbow at the inside top of the arm bone, which is not yet completely hardened in young players. Often the cartilage is also injured, which can harm the proper movement of the joint throughout life. This is why Little League has limits on the number of throws a pitcher can make (two hundred a week or ninety a game) and also tries to limit a pitcher throwing the curve ball because this motion snaps the elbow down. An injured elbow must be X-rayed, and treatment includes the **R.I.C.E.** ("Rest, Ice, Compression, and Elevation") program (see box, page 49). For little league elbow, a pitcher may have to rest the arm for six to eight weeks, or until the pain goes away. A pitcher may still play other positions and bat if this does not cause pain. Cartilage damage requires a longer period of rest and medication, and surgery is sometimes needed.

HEAD AND NECK

Head and neck injuries usually come from a player being hit by the ball. The Consumer Product Safety Commission studied the 88,700 injuries from being hit by a ball in 1995 and found that 29.5 percent of the injuries were in the head and neck. Players can also injure these areas by colliding or sliding into a base. The most dangerous head injury is a concussion, which is an injury to the brain that

ANKLE LIGAMENTS

Sprained ankles are common among baseball and softball players. They happen when the ligaments are overstretched on the outside of the ankle.

The tibia bone can be fractured during games

The end of the tibia is connected to the heel by ligaments

Strong ligaments maintain stability but can be overstretched

might cause a player to lose memory, be unconscious, or, in rare cases, die. Symptoms include a severe headache, nausea, or confusion. If a batter's helmet is damaged by a throw, the force involved could also be enough to cause a concussion. A player who is unconscious should be taken quickly to a doctor. Depending on the severity of the concussion, players will have to skip play for a minimum of seventy-two hours to about one month.

Neck injuries include those in which the nerves are stretched, which causes temporary numbness and a stinging pain, hence this injury's nickname, **stinger**. This, however, is minor in comparison to a fracture or injury involving the spinal

INJURIES AND TREATMENT

R.I.C.E.

Standing for "Rest, Ice, Compression, and Elevation," this is a treatment program most often applied to sprains and strains. The following steps should take place twenty-four to forty-eight hours after an injury.

- REST—Do not use the injured area; this may even mean bed rest. Serious injuries, such as a broken arm, require immobilization for a short period. The time needed for rest varies, depending on the injury.
- ICE—Put ice on the injured area as soon as possible. This is effective in the first two or three days. Apply ice two or three times an hour for twelve to twenty minutes each time. Use an ice pack or crushed ice in a plastic bag. Never put ice directly against the skin; wrap it in a towel and keep in place with a bandage. Alternatively, place a thin piece of cotton between the ice and skin.
- COMPRESSION—Wrap an elastic bandage snugly around the injured area, being careful not to wrap it tight enough to restrict circulation.
- ELEVATION—Raise the injured area above your heart level, if possible. You can use pillows as a prop.

The best way to relieve pain and swelling is an ice pack, seen here being applied to the wrist.

cord. A player who is lying on the ground with a serious neck injury should be moved only by qualified emergency personnel because movement could cause paralysis or death. Treatment for nonserious injuries will require a neck collar or brace, followed by exercise to strengthen the neck.

KNEE AND ANKLE

Knee injuries can occur during any action on the field. The knee's connecting tissues can be stretched or torn by a runner turning or sliding, a fielder twisting for a fly ball, or a pitcher making a delivery. A sprain is a partial or complete tear of a ligament, while a strain is the same injury to a muscle or tendon. You will know you have a sprained or strained knee if you hear a popping or snapping sound, feel pain from inside the knee, and are unable to put weight on that leg or feel that your knee is loose. The R.I.C.E. treatment will help, and players with severe injuries may have to use a splint or crutches for a while.

Cartilage injuries to the knee happen when a small piece of cartilage breaks off from the end of the bone. You will be unable to extend the leg. Other symptoms are pain, swelling, stiffness, and a catching sensation when you move. A physician will insist that you rest the knee and wear a cast for about two months. Sometimes surgery is necessary.

Ankle sprains are very common among baseball and softball players. Most twisted ankles are minor sprains, but serious sprains should be taped by a team trainer or physician. If the ankle is rested, a player can return to competition within days; but if the injury is ignored, recovery could take weeks or months. Treatment is the usual R.I.C.E. program, an ankle brace or tape, and perhaps crutches. Inflammation lasts about three days, and exercises to strengthen the ankle can begin when the player can move without pain.

INJURIES AND TREATMENT

RECOVERING FROM INJURIES

The period needed to recover from an injury depends upon how serious it is and the age and physical condition of the player. To help you stay fit as you recover, your physician will devise a rehabilitation program, such as swimming or using a stationary cycle. Specialist physical therapy or the use of ultrasound to heat the injured area may also be recommended.

Tell your physician if pain does not go away after treatment. And follow directions on adjusting your level of play or even discontinuing it. Returning to play too soon could risk another injury or aggravate the one from which you are recovering. You might need new protective equipment, such as an elbow brace or knee tape. If the previously injured area begins to hurt during a game, stop immediately. Remember, the best way to return to the diamond is to communicate and cooperate with your coach, parents, and doctor.

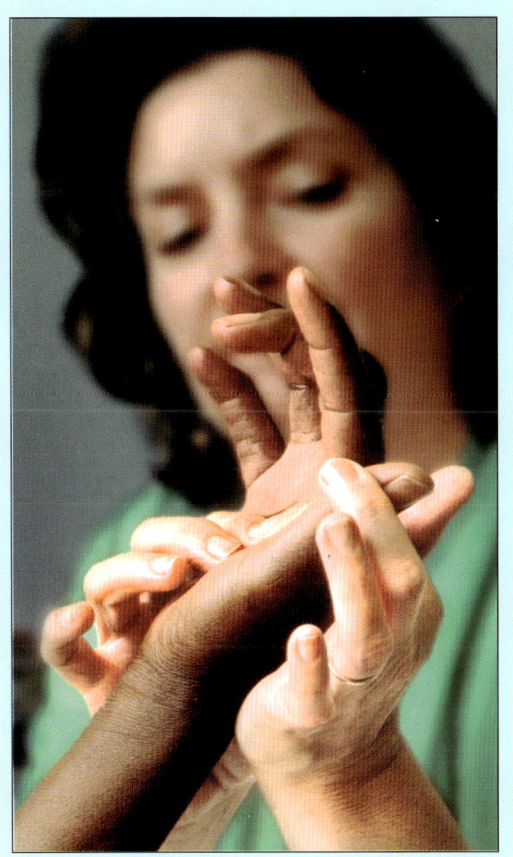

The quickest way to return to play is by following a doctor's advice, which may include physical therapy sessions.

51

Careers in Baseball

Playing baseball offers a great advantage to anyone wishing to become a professional athlete. The sport offers training and competition from the age of five, and a player can then advance through layers of increasingly difficult competition.

It is easy for a child to join a baseball or softball league. The Little League, founded in 1938, has some three million participants in baseball and softball in nearly one hundred countries. President George W. Bush is a former Little Leaguer. The League offers T-ball for children aged five to eight. Its older divisions for both baseball and softball are Little League, for those aged nine to twelve; Junior League, for ages thirteen to fourteen; Senior League, for fourteen- to sixteen-year-olds; and Big League, for those aged sixteen to eighteen. Its Challenger League is for mentally and physically disabled players from five to eighteen years old.

The Babe Ruth League, established in 1951, has nearly one million participants in its baseball and softball programs in the United States and Canada. It runs a Cal Ripken baseball league, for those aged five to twelve, and older divisions for youths thirteen to fifteen and sixteen to eighteen. The softball divisions are for those aged twelve and under, sixteen and under, and eighteen and under.

Among the other excellent youth training grounds are the Dizzy Dean and Dixie Youth leagues.

Many opportunities are available to young players who wish to participate in an organized league. Summer baseball camps also help to sharpen the skills of players who hope to make the big leagues.

"DIZZY" DEAN (1911–1974)

From 1930 to 1937, Jay Hanna "Dizzy" Dean had a brilliant pitching record with the St. Louis Cardinals. His tactics on the mound were simple: "I always just went out there and struck out all the fellows I could."

He twice led the National League in shutouts. With his younger brother, the pitcher Paul "Daffy" Dean, he won all four games for St. Louis in the 1934 World Series (each brother getting two wins). That year, his regular season record was thirty wins and seven losses.

His brilliance was ended in the 1937 All-Star game when a line drive broke his toe. He changed his pitching motion to compensate, but this injured his throwing arm. He later played for the Chicago Cubs (1938–1941) and the St. Louis Browns (1947), and became a well-known radio and TV baseball announcer. In 1953, he was elected to the Baseball Hall of Fame. Dean, who called himself "Ol' Diz," was known for his sense of humor. He once said, "Anybody who's ever had the privilege of seeing me play ball knows that I am the greatest pitcher in the world."

"Ol' Diz" said that he was the best, and his record usually supported that claim, until injuries took their toll.

CAREERS IN BASEBALL

HIGH SCHOOL PROGRAMS

Many high schools have fine baseball and softball programs. This is the place to make your mark and catch the attention of college and even professional scouts. More than 455,000 students play high school baseball, but only six out of every one hundred seniors will advance to play men's baseball on a team for a college or university of the National Collegiate Athletic Association (NCAA).

One way of increasing the chance of playing ball with your favorite college is to attend its summer baseball camp. A week's instruction may cost several hundred dollars, but this is an opportunity to meet a school's coaches, who look upon the camp as a good recruiting tool. Colleges sign many players who attend their camps.

The lessons of teamwork and sportsmanship are learned early on Little League diamonds. Here, a young pitcher prepares to pitch the ball.

Some of the best softball is played by women's teams. World championships are held by the International Softball Federation.

SCHOLARSHIPS

Colleges and universities offer baseball scholarships to the best high school players. The largest schools are in the NCAA's Division I, and they are allowed an average of 11.7 full scholarships, while the Division II programs have nine full scholarships. Some schools in both divisions do not fully fund all available scholarships. There are none offered by Division III colleges. Member schools of the National Association of Intercollegiate Athletics (NAIA) each have twelve full scholarships, and schools in the top two divisions of the National Junior College Athletic Association (NJCAA) are allowed twenty-four available full scholarships. Other programs exist, such as the Professional Baseball College Scholarship Plan, sometimes offered by major league clubs as part of a player's contract. The Babe Ruth League also has a College Scholarship Program for players who participated in its baseball and softball divisions.

College and pro scouts and even sports agents will be drawn to high school players who have the potential to be drafted by major league clubs. Most players, however, need a concerted effort to attract a college scholarship bid. Remember that failing academic grades will quickly end the dream. If you are a student

JOE DIMAGGIO (1914–1999)

Joe DiMaggio became known worldwide in 1954 for marrying Marilyn Monroe, but his real fame in America was as the "Yankee Clipper" outfielder who helped New York win ten pennants and nine World Series. The son of Italian immigrants, he joined the Yankees in 1936 and was known for his class both on and off the field.

DiMaggio was named the American League's Most Valuable Player (MVP) three times. He led the league in homers in 1937 with forty-six and—after serving in the army during World War II—in 1948 with thirty-nine. His career had many highlights, but the most remarkable was his streak of hitting safely in fifty-six consecutive games in 1941, a record that still stands. His batting average that year was .406.

Almost as remarkable was DiMaggio's ability to play with a series of injuries. When DiMaggio retired at the age of thirty-seven, he said "I was full of aches and pains." He was named to the Baseball Hall of Fame in 1955.

One of America's all-time baseball heroes, Joe DiMaggio was a quiet player who let his remarkable hitting speak for itself.

KIRK GIBSON (1957–)

When Kirk Gibson joined the Detroit Tigers in 2003 as a coach, he was returning to his hometown club. He joined the Tigers in 1979 and became an immediate star. In 1984, he helped to guide the team to the American League title, belting twenty-seven home runs. The next year, he hit twenty-nine homers and stole thirty bases in thirty-four tries. He joined the Los Angeles Dodgers in 1988 and subsequently played for the Kansas City Royals and Pittsburgh Pirates before returning to Detroit in 1993.

Injuries throughout his career never stopped Kirk Gibson, whose physical toughness was renowned. When he retired in 1995, Gibson said he had been "traded to my family."

doing well in the classroom in your junior year, send out contact letters to college coaches and also ask your high school coach to recommend you to the preferred program. By your senior year, you could phone the college coach to ask for a tryout on campus. Even if you end up making the team without the benefit of a scholarship, intercollegiate baseball is a showcase for talent and is one step closer to the professional game.

Through 2000, the major school that has won the most College World Series—the NCAA's baseball championships—was the University of Southern California (USC) with twelve; however, since 1990, Louisiana State University (LSU) has won the most, five. Texas and Arizona State have also won five over the years, and the University of Miami, Florida, has taken three titles.

The NCAA also holds a Women's College World Series for softball, which was won by the University of Arizona in 2001 and the University of California in 2002.

In all, there are more than 25,000 baseball players attending NCAA schools, and fewer than eleven of every one hundred senior players go on to be drafted by a major league team. Remember, however, that there are thirty major league teams and that these major league teams have minor league "farm" clubs, such as the teams in the Triple-A International League and Pacific Coast League, which are used to develop players.

Making it in the big leagues has long been the dream of many American children from all over the country. President Dwight Eisenhower once recalled a summer afternoon when he was a small boy fishing on a Kansas riverbank with his friend. "I told him that I wanted to be a real major-league baseball player," said Eisenhower. "My friend said he'd like to be President of the United States. Neither of us got our wish."

Glossary

Aerobic: Describes any exercise that demands increased oxygen, thereby forcing up the heart rate and breathing.

ASA: Abbreviation for the Amateur Softball Association, the national governing body of softball in the United States.

Bullpen: The place on the side of the field where relief pitchers warm up during a game.

Bunt: A play in which the batter strikes the ball with a loosely held bat and no swing to keep the ball in the infield.

Cartilage: Strong connective tissue found in the body's joints and other structures. Children have a higher percentage of cartilage than adults, some of which turns to bone as they grow older.

Curveball: A pitch in which the ball swerves because of a spin put on it during the delivery.

Double play: A play in which the defense manages to put out two players.

Dugout: A low shelter that contains the players' bench and faces the baseball diamond.

Hamstrings: The group of three muscles set at the back of the thigh.

Ligament: A short band of tough body tissue that connects bones or holds together joints.

Little league elbow: Injury to the arm and sometimes the cartilage near the elbow, due to overuse.

Overuse injury: An injury caused by repeating the same action many times.

R.I.C.E.: An injury treatment program of rest, ice, compression, and elevation.

GLOSSARY

Rotator cuff: A capsule of tendons and muscles that holds the shoulder joint in place, enabling the rotational movement of the arm.

Rounders: An English game from which baseball developed.

Stinger: A neck injury caused by stretched nerves.

Strike zone: The area through which a pitched baseball must pass to be called a strike. For baseball, this is from the knees to the chest of a batter.

Tendonitis: Inflammation and pain in the tendons.

Tendon: A body tissue, also called a sinew, that connects muscles to bones.

Ultrasound: Sound waves that are outside the range of human hearing. Physical therapists sometimes use ultrasound machines to treat damaged muscles by sending the sound waves vibrating through the injured area.

Visualization: The technique of improving sports performance by imagining yourself in a future action, such as a baseball play.

Further Information

USEFUL WEB SITES

Babe Ruth League: www.baberuthleague.org

For baseball equipment, try: www.baseball-and-gear.com

High School Baseball Web: www.hsbaseballweb.com

Little League: www.littleleague.org

Amateur Softball Association: www.softball.org

U.S.A. Baseball: www.usabaseball.com

The Web sites listed on this page were active at the time of publication. The publisher is not responsible for Web sites that have changed their address or discontinued operation since the date of publication. The publisher will review and update the Web sites upon each reprint.

FURTHER READING

Briand, Keven and Buck Martinez. *The Baseball Book: A Young Player's Guide to Baseball.* Westport, Connecticut: Firefly Books Ltd., 2003.

Mintzer, Richard. *The Everything Kids' Baseball Book: Star Players, Great Teams, Baseball Legends, and Tips on Playing Like a Pro.* Holbrook, Massachusetts: Adams Media Corporation, 2001.

Monteleone, John and Deborah Crisfield. *The Louisville Slugger Complete Book of Women's Fast-Pitch Softball.* New York: Henry Holt, 1999.

Roberts, Robin. *Sports Injuries.* Brookfield, Connecticut: Millbrook Press, 2001.

Torres, John Albert. *Top 10 Baseball Legends.* Berkeley Heights, New Jersey: Enslow Publishers, 2000.

FURTHER INFORMATION

THE AUTHOR

Dr. John D. Wright is a writer and journalist with many years of experience. He has been a reporter for *Time* and *People* magazines, a journalist for the U.S. Navy, and reported for newspapers in Alabama and Tennessee. He holds a Ph.D. degree in Communications from the University of Texas, and has taught journalism at colleges in Alabama and Virginia. He now lives in Herefordshire, England.

THE CONSULTANTS

Susan Saliba, Ph.D., is a senior associate athletic trainer and a clinical instructor at the University of Virginia in Charlottesville, Virginia. A certified athletic trainer and licensed physical therapist, Dr. Saliba provides sports medicine care, including prevention, treatment, and rehabilitation for the varsity athletes at the University. Dr. Saliba holds dual appointments as an Assistant Professor in the Curry School of Education and the Department of Orthopaedic Surgery. She is a member of the National Athletic Trainers' Association's Educational Executive Committee and its Clinical Education Committee.

Eric Small, M.D., a Harvard-trained sports medicine physician, is a nationally recognized expert in the field of sports injuries, nutritional supplements, and weight management programs. He is author of *Kids & Sports* (2002) and is Assistant Clinical Professor of Pediatrics, Orthopedics, and Rehabilitation Medicine at Mount Sinai School of Medicine in New York. He is also Director of the Sports Medicine Center for Young Athletes at Blythedale Children's Hospital in Valhalla, New York. Dr. Small has served on the American Academy of Pediatrics Committee on Sports Medicine for the past six years, where he develops national policy regarding children's medical issues and sports.

Index

Page numbers in *italics* refer to photographs and illustrations.

Amateur Softball Association (ASA) 19, 21
American League 11, 17, 27, 58
ankle injuries 32, 43, *48*, 50

Babe Ruth League 14, 53, 56, 62
base, stealing 15, *16*, 27, 58
baseball
    history 9–14
    rules 9, 10, 14, 16, 17
bats 14, 22, *23*, 41
Brett, George 27
Brooklyn Dodgers 13, 15

career development *52*, 53, 55, 56, 59
chest protectors *34*, 37–8
coaches 55, 59
colleges 55, 56, 59
curve balls 31, 47

Dean, Jay Hanna "Dizzy" 13, 54
Detroit Tigers 13, 58
DiMaggio, Joe 11, 57
Dixie Youth Baseball 38, 40, 53
Doubleday, Abner 9–10

Eisenhower, President Dwight 59
equipment
    balls 14, 22, *23*, 35
    bats 14, 22, *23*, 41
    protective *34*, 36–40
exercises
    after injury 50, 51
    conditioning 32–3
    stretching *24*, 28, *29*, 30
    warming up 28, *29*, 30–2

face masks *34*, 37, 38–9
footwear 36, 38
fractures 31, 45, 47

Gibson, Kirk 58
gloves 35, 37, 40 *see also* mitts

Hancock, George 19–20
head injuries 43, 47–8
helmets *34*, 37, 38, *39*

injuries
    ankles 32, 43, *48*, 50
    avoiding *24*, 25–33, 43
    back 17, 32, 48, 50
    cartilage 47, 50
    catchers 36–7, 38, *42*
    fractures 31, 45, 47
    head 43, 47–8
    knees 17, 43, 50
    overuse 45–7
    pitchers 35–6, 46, 47
    R.I.C.E. treatment 47, 49, 50
    shoulders 43, 45–7
    sprains 32, *48*, 50
    tendonitis 27, 45–6
International Softball Federation (ISF) 21, *56*

Kansas City Royals 27, 58
Karros, Eric *8*
knee injuries 17, 43, 50

Little League 14, 31, 35–6, 47, 53, *55*
Los Angeles Dodgers *8*, 58
McGwire, Mark 13, 17, *25*
mental preparation 25–8
mitts *34*, 37 *see also* gloves
motivation 25–8
muscles
    hamstrings *31*, 32
    shoulders 30, 46
    stretching *24*, 28, *29*, 30
    see also injuries

National Association of Professional Baseball Players 10–11
National Baseball Hall of Fame 9, 15, 27, 54
National Collegiate Athletic Association (NCAA) 55, 56, 59
National League of Professional Base Ball Clubs 11, 13, 15
National Softball Hall of Fame 21
New York Giants 13–14
New York Yankees 11, 12, 14, 57

Olympic Games *13*, 14, *18*, 21
outs 16, 17, 22
overuse injuries 45–7

pain 43, 46–7, 50, 51
physical preparation 28, *29*, 30–3
physical therapy 47, 51
positive thinking 25–8
preparation
    mental 25–8
    physical 28, *29*, 30–3
    see also training
protective equipment *34*, 36–40

Rest, Ice, Compression, and Elevation (R.I.C.E.) treatment 47, 49, 50
Robinson, Jackie 13, 15
rounders 9
rules
    baseball 9, 10, 14, 16, 17
    softball 21, 22, *23*
Ruth, George Herman "Babe" 11, 12

scholarships 56, 59
school programs 55–6
shin guards *34*, 37, 38
slang 44
softball 9, *18*, 19–22, *23*, 53, *56*, 59
St. Louis Cardinals 13, 17, 54
stretching *24*, 28, *29*, 30
surgery 17, 47, 50

tendonitis 27, 45–6
throat protectors *34*, 37
training 32–3
    after injury 50, 51
    camps *52*, 55
    see also preparation

universities 55, 56, 59

visualization 25–8

warming up 28, *29*, 30–2
World Series 11, 14, 15, 17, 27, 54, 57
Wrigley Field, Chicago *10–11*